MUSAFIR MUSINGS

SCRIBBLES OF LOVE, LIGHT AND LIFE

SAYAN DEY

To people, near and far, who have touched upon my life, in everyway.

Contents

Contents

Preface

As long as you feel pain, you're still alive. As long as you make mistakes, you're still human. And as long as you keep trying, there' still hope." - Susan Gale

As an academic trying hard to clear the clutter in head, there is none better to take life lessons than life itself. The everyday chores, the mundane musings, the moments which weave magic; all these are cues to be taken up. There are times we feel strange and weird about being alive, even best of us have gone through such train wrecks. Its life that comes to rescue again. Pats back on your shoulder and reverberates "you will be fine! Just not today"

And the curtains go off again! The show resumes.

This is a collection of short passages from everyday journey called life, in its full manifesto.

The mystery called 'Life'

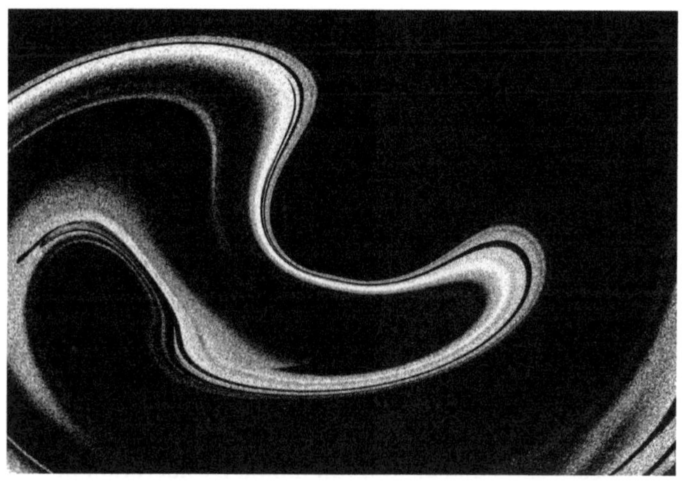

Nature rolls on the Praxis of action and reaction, cause and effect, often! But what about casualties sans cause! Effect without explanation? Aren't they squally? Aren't they foul?

All our life we hustle for dignity deeds and distinctions. Unrelenting elbow grease for an opening out of claustrophobia, sweat for sanction. Sanction of solace!

Life doesn't comfort us with incognito mode. Rather it perturbs and lefts us parched. Many spirits are done just there just like that. Sordid God-speed.

Still there is more to fall than just caterwauling. A rise for royalty, a rise for respect. A life can be lived in eclipse but death should bring out full moon. Desideration of Godhead!

One Last Time

Gloomy days hound dark nights

Insomnia pouring deep in aching fights

The forgotten road, the mirage delights

Spent debugging the navigation in fading lights

The struggle intensifying each day

Efforts to numbness in sheer dismay

The calling in sway, knocked off in array

The Frey gutted deep in fray

The canvas pale and agonisingly grey

The milestones in torment

The voyage in entanglement

The destination San destiny

The shattered cardiac, in pieces, tiny

The star out casted and lost

The dreams that did cost

The climax is in, end of a filthy mime

But I dare again, to yearn for you; one last time...

One Last Time!

Love Comes Softly

And some stories end for a new beginning! Although life doesn't possess rewind button but you can always fix some notches just like a tape! An analog anomaly!

The bewildering traits of troglodyte mind are beyond fanciest fancies! We sometimes defy rationale and aspire to pull up magic! How illusive it may seem.

Like phoenix we rise from the ashes! Gather ourselves from dust! With Strom in breath and volcano in heart! We press the paddle again. The gas meter touching zero ! With burning love in veins (oh Presley)

We can run, hide but we can't escape! Because of all the gin joints in all of the town and may be in entire universe!

You get a knock ever subtly. And she is there!

Rugged, dusty and dirty! She takes you back! Her tightly pressed lips shivering in unexplainable emotions! She blinks and rekindles the lost flame! Just like that

Love comes softly! And you sink for a rise!

Twisted Yet Treasured

They had issues...plenty of them since inception.

He was always into her; truly, madly, deeply! Ever since his eyes met her the very first time. She was perhaps more shrewd, expedient and conniving of the two.

Perhaps the troglodyte inside him was tailored into a more humanoid form! Courtesy; those pair of bright eyes! A smile that would iron out wrinkles inside out. Yes she was an Iris for him.

He was not the worst person you would come across! Yeah a bit rusty, resentful and might be a little non-sensical at times! Well that's obvious when he had been knocked out hard many a times before. A soft, goodie-goodie boy got galvanised into robust robot, mechanical yet mellow!

Now that their fling died a premature death, off course he has to be pinned for the rift, she can't be given a clean whistle either. May be his mechanical cardiac revolted against his mean wills and he decided to let her go. He loved her enough to prompt her freeway!

He sincerely wanted her to be happy, smiling forever! He had put his effort so much not to see her moist in tears because of him, he ended up smashing his longings and belongings for her! Intentionally and knowingly! He set her free! To take everything head on with an agonising smile inside out. He did.

Now he seems to be turned into an old, ghostly creature! All alone and mourning! It kills him thinking her with other guy! Still an illusory glimpse of her beats his heart at the rate of knots! His gaze still follows her till she disappears in crowd! May be deep down he still feels for her! Strange and weird! One of a kind! Love takes it all! Beyond dominant narratives! Some tales are twisted yet treasured; for lifetime!

To, Life, light and love!

We all had been a part of that uncanny love story that we think now, we better have parted. But nemesis doesn't knock with an embargo. Till the time you realise, you are drowned for the good, bad and the ugly. We all had that blurry face in our mind that we never stopped thinking about. We all had that imperfect sketch we kept on scribbling without contour. We all had that scar we hide, we nurse but we couldn't get rid of. We all had that zero point for which we could run for miles with gas meter blinking nil. Love is a magic comfort food for the faint hearted. We all had risked love. We did and see now! We're lonely ghost of a man. It doesn't mean that we're never going to get hurt again, but the pain we feel will never compare to the regret that comes from walking away from love. And from someone who's felt a lot of both, trust us, pain beats regret every day of the week and twice on Sunday. Don't run away. Don't do it. And if this is the way things turn out then this is not what life is meant to be!

The PERIOD

I walked on a lonely road

I did everything I felt just

I went the extra mile every instance

I questioned my action, conscience...cardiac

I doubted myself

I tried to forge the parallels

I urged to converge

I pacified the author

I crucified the speaker

Running after a merry mirage

A reel that never merged with real

After all of these, I realised it's not worth

If it's life, Life should not be like this

A rebel without a cause

A fighter without foundation

The last punch should be for self

A gasp to suck the air, a fall for the rise

PERIOD!

We Live, We Learn

Life is a school beyond comprehensiveness. The more you learn, more meager you feel about your learning. Are we right always? The decisions we take, the thought process that goes about it, the rationale and justification of the same. There are moments of hesitancy, train-wreck and quicksand! We fall, we commit mistakes! None can predict what's coming next and we dont even have iota of clue regarding how shall we react. But we live. We learn. The more we learn, more meager we feel about our learning.

No Honks, When Love Leaves

How weird it feels to confront your former fling when your entire entity simply refuses to accept her untimely disappearance? A part of her still kicking him inside, alive and well! How does he tackle all these?

He always had the notion, in any relationship power lies with one who cares less! The one who is not afraid of loss! One who is calling the shots all the time! One who holds the brickbat and cold as a carcass!

Now, it's awfully late when he realises that he was so very wrong! Power in a relationship lies with one who cares more! The unconditional care actually sets the hierarchy! The flow of attachment. The hypo tone in relation. Now he realises sometimes he should have risked! Risked his heart, his love! All this while he kept on thinking what if she had left him? What if she had hurt him? The fear of presumed solitude actually pushed him to solitary confinement in actuality! The fear won over his emotions!

He now feels, she might be thinking in the same line as he does. The hopelessly hopeful moron! Some 40 years down the line, both of them would be sitting in a park babysitting their grandchildren and thinking what if they had given themselves a chance? A risk of losing; he feels so!

No pain in the world is equitable to the regret that comes from walking away from someone, whom you loved truly, deeply and madly! And what's more ironical is you still do and seems you will have a tough time erasing the same! May be you won't be able to either!

That's how love comes! Softly and silently! And when it leaves there is no honk either! It leaves you like a subconscious dream! And when you realise; the damage is done! The dent is beyond repair....

Love Enough to Let Go

And his soul still claustrophobic under the debris of bygone days! But situations are up in ante to play a cruel game of numbness! He broke down in pieces she would never be able to tally, he gasps for few moments of respite only to find haunted by her memories.

He tries hard to battle inside out! Fake a smile, adorning All Is Well attitude! Alas! Who knows what he is going through! A sense of loss which seems irreparable, an incomprehensible void that electrocutes him all through, a sin he never committed but accepting all odds as a passive, docile Zombie, literally!

He's not Revenant, he is not a dead man walking, he's not a pool which will bury dead !

A ghostly, lonely man left to destiny; necropolis cacophonies!

A homosepian; who loved, who loved her enough to let her go, Just eyeing her happiness!

All real stories do not meet a reel like ending! Some don't! It's just the end of a beginning that starts!

'Power' Ties

So who does hold the key in a tie? Who navigates the power dynamics in a correlation? The obvious answer goes for a toss in oblivion. It does. All throughout the quest of adulation we all have at some point of time vetoed the powerful over powerless, the command over composure, haven't we? Seldom have we tended to look beyond narratives and norms. But trust life, it has uncanny way driving home the less motored aspects. Just tender your best feasible intention and let it go. Just like that. You will experience a never before curtain being raised upon thyself. A state of bliss you longed for, a destiny which may seem San material union but having contours of liberation you long yearned for. The power lies with the one who can let go, unconditionally what s/he once embraced in hope not knowing that hope is a hopeless and hyped hypothesis.

Déjà Vu of love that is lost

Déjà Vu of love that is lost! Majority of illuminated minds would strike off this hypothetical proposition as sub normality of a hallucinating mind! And your troglodyte self cannot but to accept their ever gripping logic and sense! And they crucify your belief as illusive and having contours of mirage. And you are done, just like that!

But who are we to thump on our faculties of being the Alpha And Omega in the taxonomical array? As and when fate decides to knock you out! Courtesy the twist and turns you never saw coming!

And his eyes got glued in her blue *bindi*! He even skipped his mundane chores for a moment or two! Her 6 feet long stitched venture made him fall for her again! Just like the first day! The ethnic drape of colors bluish red to red in hue, of medium to high lightness, and of low to moderate saturation made her look like Iris, the goddess of rainbow!

Didn't she resemble the silhouette he has been chasing all these nights, weeks and months? Yes! She did resemble every bit of it! A part of her is still alive in him, kicking and giggling! The more he tried to bury her thoughts he sank more, in her musings, always vivid and full of chrome.

Like a dead duck he was forgetful of the fact that he should also be mindful or her gaze! Is she too willing to rekindle the lost flame or it was just an illusion of his mortal eyes! Was he encroaching her space or his space was always there? His work was cut out to sort all these and more! But he failed, he failed miserably.

It is most likely be an illusion in the end! He is very well aware of it. But it mattered least to him at that very moment! All his life he believed this day to be of Aphrodite's too while lion's share being devoted to goddess of wisdom and knowledge! And the irony is even in his bizarre wilderness he never thought this would ever grip him again for the nemesis ! The nemesis he cherished in her eyes all these while. A deep sink like the quicksand! All he knew he was in love again, at least at that moment.

Requiem for a Dream

Dreams do come true. Sometimes consciously, you wish them to be, sometimes you don't. But irrespective of all these competing variables, life with its unpredictable set of integration and differentiation provide us with solutions, often in a surprising quantum.

Reminiscence

He had never felt that something which has been called over and out can kept coming around like a boomerang. Something which has been written off can be of exceptional recurring value. He has been of the view all this time that it's not that hard to go along the flow when the voyage has been abandoned, the destination has been done away with.

And, he was wrong, so very wrong. Reminiscence does go for a total recall, and retained impressions of bitter-sweet nodes haunt like a bounty hunter; with one's subsistence becomes too uncomfortable to be comforted. Occasionally, stealing a look out of an inadvertent crossover, a sudden flash of cell notification pulse which reminds him there is still a humanoid crawling within; making his presence felt with feeble fists forcing the untimely thumps in cardiac walls. The cruel destiny laughs out loud plotting those moments, every single time. And a part of him dies in a drop of hat, just like that; over and over again.

What he does not pay a heed to, or rather pretends to be, is sharp mound of soreness soaring inside, a tempest which tempts tumultuous twinge, a ripper which rips him straight through busting his sense of self like a sledgehammer and cuts him into halves! And even he can't deny a bleeding heart, a compassion which is set for a reluctant reincarnation.

The 'Joker' in us

Myriad of emotions that define life could have been a wonderful addition to existing base of comprehensibility but is left as a incomprehensive, dark and enigmatic metaphor beyond objectivity. This is antithesis, ridiculed by power structures and facilities. The game does not end here but rings a bell! Within all of us, at some point in life.

Between a yes and a no, between the good and the evil, between the god and the satan ; there is much more! The merging metaphors and harsh realities often make us a villain in someone else's story. All of us !

We all are insecure clown on medication for pseudobulbar affect (PBA) which makes one to continual, involuntary, exaggerated display of laughter , cry or other emotions disconnected from real life situations. And here we laughs, uncontrollably, even when in tears, even when we are fuming within !

Isolated, rejected and failed, we are mentally ill loners with a society that abandons us and treats us like trash?

Life dwells in hyperreality of multiple tracks where the we as Jokers walk across stages and perform with elan with no fear of consequences. We acts, We live the characters as everready to jump platforms.

Life puts up a scary show and all we are left with, moist eyes and a stiff smile. Such is the Joker and his Jokes.

Unpredictable and uncanny.

Joker makes us love the antagoinst in each one us! The dark side in each one of us. It's leaves you a thought what if antithesis were not the way they are! What if genesis and nemesis could exchange tables?

Strangers

Really, strangers are here, there and everywhere to knock us for a loop! They do! It's startling to experience how strangers, at varied crossroads in our life lead us to discover umpteen undisclosed territories within one! There are conversations, both readable and audible; there are conquests, both overt and covert! There are subtle musings San concrete black and white, with hues of dark grey diffusing! There have been junctures, recurring, which had the might to dethrone us out of our comforts; at times paving in contrasting comforts! All in courtesy strangers! They cut across limits of permeability, thresholds of vulnerability! The equation appears inequitable! Strange indeed! You are in a fix how to achieve equilibrium! The very idea is unequal as it surpasses finest theories of chemical kinetics with ignorant ease! Wonder what chemicals mind secret at the first place!

Still as long as strangers are there, life has a chance, of mutating, off course either way ! At least it will have the humanoid disrobed, in its basic premise ! An interesting idea to ponder over if not panic!

Comprehensive Incomprehensibility

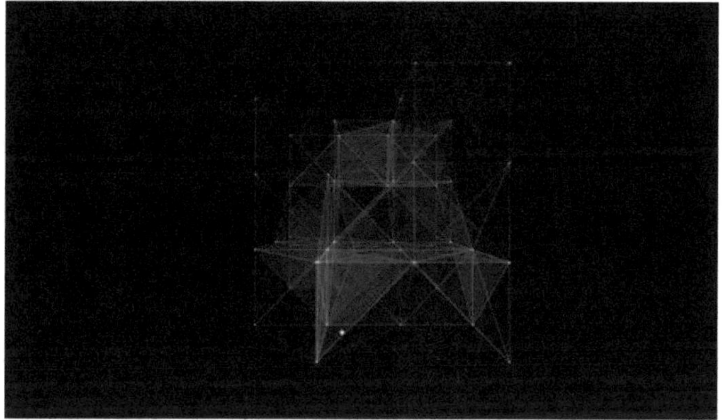

We feel claustrophobic, Puzzles remain mysteries like Rubik, more you push, the more you sink, Quicksand shadows quicksilver, An eclipse that seems never ending, reel never merges with real, it's just an illusion, of self, of mirror !

Time, a great leveler

In the end time is a great leveler. Indeed it is one of the cruelest entity in human evolution. Quicksand it is. The hard you tend to grip it, it slips. And you sink too. But the greatest virtue that we possess as greatest creation of Omni is to wait for the tables to turn. It does. Patience paves way to peace. Deeds are rewarded, misdeeds miscarriage. The invisible law of nature balances it all. The grave you dig today welcomes you tomorrow! You fall, inevitably. And Yes! In the end it doesn't even matter

Pensive Even Amidst Pessimism

I miss my prowess of getting pensive even amidst pessimism. I remember being a kid who was exposed to novels and fictions at an early age may be when I was 9 or 10. The words had me, for the rest of my sustenance. It gave me so much beyond pseudo intelligence and hyped knowledge we seek in confined set ups. I must say they have this tremendous power of teleportation. Many a times I travelled in heights of Kanchenjunga and slept in sleeping bags, I had an encounter with an old but desperate man eater in the grass jungles; I had solved a murder mystery in Gangtok and so on with them, my accomplices from the prints. I could travel through meadows of Meghalaya in early winter morning with dew drops trickling down the window, with chilly breeze soothing your diminishing hair lines, thick blanket of fog down the hill hand beckons you to unknown, may be to the mystery land under Earth's crust.

Being Mature

We should be mature. Yes that's the bottom-line for sustenance in this time of crisis. But does that ask you to be indifferent or having a sense of hibernation towards the stimulus out around you. Are we not alive enough to go beyond normative narrations and churn the obvious reasons with a childish enthusiasm? Shall not we be affected by emotional, psychological and spiritual aspects that make us more than lump of flesh and blood? Is that a crime to be sensitive with the knowledge that it has flip side too, of knocking you off from your comfort confinement. May be being able to see and pass is a greater virtue than see and act. Finally you are called matured only when you become deaf, dumb and blind!

It Rains on

Its flabbergasting to experience a day of unrelenting pour, gesture of contumacious clouds in a Cimmerian sky! The thick drizzles usher in innumerable chromes in one's mind; black, white and the dots of grey in between. Memories flash like the ever zippy lightning in a rain drenched field; the good, bad and the ugly.

The dormant hours especially post noon are quite something! They let out the poet, the writer and what not in thee! Everything you ever wanted to be! Most importantly they let the humanoid out of you! In its disrobed avatar! Something you can see through! The YOU that you can trust, you can converse San pleasantries.

The YOU, you have been searching all throughout. The YOU who was lost in mundane chores of sustenance. The YOU who was shadowed under cosmetic mask all this time.

Sometimes, you may feel vulnerable too in these enervated hours. The moment of mortifications when you no longer able to get away from YOU. The abstract advisement transcends into forms or maybe short shrift that bamboozles!

So what are you left with? Thoughts, thoughts and more thoughts. Like the drips which make you wet but you can't hold onto them! They slip like quick sand! Thoughts pitch in, in numbers and fade out too! And the pour keeps on ticking in thy cardiac chronograph! And it rains on.

Compatibility and Commitment

They say compatibility is an issue in commitment! Ask them whether Sun had it when he was in osculation with earth for the first time! Unaware of the fact that he eventually burnt out the tender earth. Did earth complain? She awaits for him still! The dawn sets the stage again. For burning love! And the love to burn.

Parched in Pour

The darkness reigned in, sky erupted

Covert deliberations deluged

Cardiac chords unplugged

The epitome numb, soul plagued

Demonic darkness pitches in

Ally of necropolis cacophony and tormenting pain

The Road Less Motored

And, I choose the road less motored

After last joint; flummoxed and bored

The perturbed I shy away from skyscrapers

I press the gas, a misfit in the mob of go-getters

And I choose the road less motored

By the deep woods and clear blue sky

Following trails of Albatross scaling high

The bumpy ride takes me countryside

Where horizons meet; side by side

And I choose the road less motored

The kaleidoscope unfolds far in the cloud

The Cascade in my veins regains roar and loud

The fuel meter alarmingly shivers to nil

I go overdrive! With 'Burning Love' to refill

And I chose the road less motored

The sun mellows down its grandeur

Soothing breeze rolls down the mercury meter

The fading light in anticipation of his queen

Who comes glittering out of her dark reign?

The silent whispers humming along

As I retrieve the way back lone and prolong

Another Sunday that least mattered

And I choose the road less motored!

The Conversations

So the conservations started!

Early in the morning, late in the night and virtually whenever they had slightest moments of leisures! Actually, leisure hours became the forerunners surpassing their mundane schedule!

Well, he was not a prince born with silver spoon nor he could hibernate in a utopian island in his dreams. He was a mango people like all of us! A mediocre student battling it out to churn out the survival strategies! He had responsibilities, aspirations of his parents and his own will to lead a life a few notches above average!

She on the other hand hailed from a backdrop which was more affluent than him, at least! She was studying for sure but Sans any definite goal, because she had this neck for employing people, thorough genetic permutations and that was what in which she found her true calling.

But, unequal lovers in every sense shunned their prejudices and decided to live out loud in love!

Soon he found out that his pocket money was draining like first drops of rain in desert! Even the tariff cutters could not stop the cutting of cutting edge hole in his wallet! So he tried to be smart! Well all this while he was in hallucination that he was street smart and can pursue anything, anyone as per his likings!

He: Listen, I remain so very busy in field during day time and evenings are occupied with desk works. I will call you at around 11 every night and we will talk for an hour or so. We both need good naps after tiring days. And since things are going perfect between us, why to stay glued to the phone 24*7. This is childish. We can move forward our things in a matured fashion.

A couple of minutes silence followed his verse. He did set the agenda and seeing her silence he started thinking "oh that was easy! I could make her understand. She will be agreeing everyway"

Just as when Mr. Confident was overconfident about the outcome of his influential speech.....

She: (Sighs) Ok. As you say! But meet me once for 2 minutes tomorrow evening. I will be calling you while returning from class.

The next day they did not talk for entire day. A bit unusual for him too, it seemed. Something missing, he was not habituated to. Anyway he was content that he has resolved the matter in his own style!

In the evening,

She: Where are you?

He: Started for office

She: Well, I am done with class. Meet me at the junction where you take auto for the office.

He: Okay, but anything urgent? Actually I am late. Can we do this tomorrow?

She: 2 minutes? Is that too much?

He: (clearly embarrassed) well, ok. I am coming.

After 10 minutes......

She hands him a small packet wrapped well all around.

He: What is this? I don't like this fashion of gifting.

She : (Smiling) Nothing . Go to work. I don't want to take the blame for your firing order!

Curious he couldn't restrain his penchant for unlocking the mystery, tears apart the packet just as when he sits in an auto.

What's in!

A SIM card of the network she subscribes!

He rings her back!

He: I guess you have mistakenly left your Sim card to me. What am I supposed to do with this?

She: (calm but firm intonation) Insert it in the other slot. From today you need not to call. Whenever you are free and willing, a missed call is all what I expect. I will revert you.

He was red faced by now and somewhere down the line his masculinity must have gone for a quite toss.

He: (Helplessly) was it that necessary? I could have managed the Sim if you had asked me for it.

She: (swallows slang halfway) you did what you could and I did what I found necessary. Stop lecturing me and work. And call me after office. If I don't see my screen flashing by 11 tonight, even your boss can't save you. I love you; I love you enough to kill you too, if needed. Take Care.

He hangs up. A tight lipped smile slowly disturbs the evenness of his cheeks. His ever so faint whispers fade in airwaves! But it keeps on echoing within...." Endless Love"

Ode to Oddity

Perched, the quest unending

The silence impenetrably deafening

The cauldron void

The vital signs devoid

The ever drizzling drips

The memories, soul rips

The cold shiver down the spine

End appears ominous, ornamented canine

The mistake, if ever it was

Only unconditional affection! Alas

Beaten to death, faith crucified

Talks of vindication, I am pacified

Amused in barbed wire confinement

Joyous in lone regiment

Thy happiness is ramifications

Of my post-truth reflections!

Some reflections are anti-rhetorical!

He is reminiscing the day they had their first conversation! He felt a special connect, an unexplainable sink! He never felt anything like that before...

He was quick to react! He knew the signs; writings on the wall had 'ominous' written all over them! He tried his best to run away! Consoled his cardiac like a pro nanny! But the stubborn pump machine revolted! May be it was rejoicing the new pastures unlikely its owner! So it revolted!

She entered like an Iris, the goddess of Rainbow and left like an endearing mirage! Some reflections are anti-rhetorical!

Now, it seems he is acquiring more of her chromes and she reciprocating aptly! He is reaching emotional peaks and she achieving calmness of a morgue room! Too practical. The exchange of courts are paradoxical to the narrative that was ought to mature!

She did nail him! Six feet under! Many a times and the final nail did come from her armor too! But he can't blame her even! It was him who handed her that special license, because he loved her more than anyone else in this world.

He still remembers her! In solitary nights, his hibernating den transcends into an arena where bitter-sweet memories of her marquees like a reel venture! He relives those and wipes of moist cheeks! Men never cry! Even then his heart sends sacks of good wishes to her planting an imaginary kiss to her airy forehead! And he remains there....murmuring...ever so softly..."accept them”

They call it breakups!

And even discarding minuscule 160 characters of lower limit...the late night text read " it's over ! I think we can't pull it anymore"

What more did he need after an underperformed day at GD-PI table! A kiosk of mixed emotion ran through arteries! All he could type and delete in recurring "why"

Well, hiccups don't come with a Suhel Seth manual! Survival strategies seem vague! Justification seems blurry and rationale appears shallow!

The pain rips your cardiac chambers into numbers even ruminants will envy! The inexpressible expressions make you heavy! A mound of bitter truth hard to swallow! A lump of agony that defies solute-solvent principle! A prick that hurts more than a lethal shell!

They call it breakups! Wonder what remains rooted after that torment! What keeps you kicking when the leg-ends for your legend! What keeps you going when it's tough even to crawl?

Its life that comes to rescue. Pats back on your shoulder and reverberates "you will be fine! Just not today"

And the curtains go off! The show resumes.

A meet to remember

And the untimely cacophony of the mobile sliced through the silent October morning! The hallucination was shattered into pieces!

5-15 it was! He cursed himself for not putting the phone into hibernation.

The dizzy eyes refused to pay attention to incoming! The hands obliged with reluctance.

He :Hello

She: My bus has reached.

He: Good. Go home. Get a good sleep

As he was about to hung up

She screamed: Did I call you in these wee hours to get your advice?

He: What's wrong now! Autos will be in any minute

She: To hell with your autos! I want to see you right now

He: Are you nuts? Its 5-15. We can meet in the morning, afternoon evening whenever you say! Please not now

She: You are coming! Or I am sitting here till my parents put a missing FIR

He: you are crazy! Insane! I am not coming

She: hope you heard me well

He: the entrance is locked. The key is in other room where others are in deep sleep.

She: I don't know anything! I am here after two months. And I don't want to see anyone else before you

He: Wish I knew that I will have to entertain tantrums of a psycho girl

She: Now you do!

He knew he lost all hands up. He won't be able to escape without escaping the bed! He got up and reincarnated the spy self of him to nab the keys like light rays in vacuum!

He walked, he was almost up to his breath as he covered 500 meters in less than a minutes!

There she was! Rugged, dusty, sleepy after overnight journey! But she refused to give up her smile.

He went forward! In a track pant, a T-shirt and a slipper! He was not sure that's attire you find a man adorning when he is going to confront his lady love after a span of 60 days! It mattered a little to her! She hugged! He hugged! They hugged!

Merely for iota of seconds! She couldn't meet his eyes after that!

She: I am sorry! I broke your sleep! I was dying to see you

He: it was worth (smiling)

What they didn't notice is that the sunrays kissed earth for the first time in the day!

Because it's 'you'

And it happens! Not once, not twice, as many times we fall, we rise.

As many times we are Ready to bear the brunt, to carry the bruises, to shatter into pieces, cure the ache and dare again!

It happens! You know how it feels, you have been through all this, nothing new, nothing unexplored but still we dare because it's 'you'

The Longing

And he refreshed the home screen!

A red dot flashed in the friend-zone! Another one, he just thought and ignored.

His mind and heart filled with a smiling face, ponytails, embroidered *Patiala!* All he could think was the moment she stood up and responded the attendance call! Actually the name to be precise the surname had made him twist his torso acute angled to see the homecoming!

There she was! Bright eyes under cautious care of spectacle, a dimple that would cut six inches deep unless you happen to possess a blood pumping arrangement only! If one has a heart she would have dig deep in just like her depreciation in cheeks!

All engrossed in her musings, he checked the list of incomings! A routine check!

Hell no! Mercy! She it was! Right out of the screws! It was her untimely appearance that he was longing since time.

Rest is life

Eyes met, they paused...

Eye to eye...

May be for a fraction of second

But...

The moment was momentous with flashing memories...

The conversations, The silent peeps, the tight lipped talks, the silent whispers for being together, the brawls, the good, bad and ugly...

All and sundry...

One moment all it took

Then...they went on normally

Rather pretended to be...

Rest is life

The eclipse was over!

And they paused!

Her eyes glued on his subtle stubble! And he froze in her eyes.

Clock kept on ticking in its merry way! To them it seemed to be eternity, relativity of time was just an anomaly here!

They looked at each other! A cold wave ran through his spine! She felt a shiver up through her torso!

They tried hard to restrain! Alas, quicksand it was. The more you try the more you sink!

Moments passed by! They didn't care! All they knew was a fall. A fall to rise! A narrative ran till climax in those pair of eyes!

The eclipse was over! They were in love

Grown Up

How it feels to be grown up! Many fancy it asserting that it gives you autonomy as a person! Power, freedom, choice and empowerment! But have we thought what it costs to us? Your guts will be spilled out cause you will be locking horns with unequal enemies! Still you never complain or precisely you ought not to! Push back your bloody guts inside again get ready for another sucker punch! You will have to fake a smile even you are dead duck! You need to appear gutsy when you are broken inside out! You need to get on with the game even when you want a retirement! You need to pull and push hard when you are tired and need some breathing space! You are not supposed to act naive even when claustrophobic ventilation goes off beam with Godspeed! Cause you are grown up.

Printed by Libri Plureos GmbH in Hamburg, Germany